RIDERS ON THE WIND

RIDERS
ON THE WIND

Laurence Swinburne

Illustrated by Dan Hubrich

629.13
SW1
8878

Blairsville Junior High School
Blairsville, Pennsylvania

RAINTREE PUBLISHERS
Milwaukee • Toronto • Melbourne • London

Library of Congress Number: 79-21190

2 3 4 5 6 7 8 9 0 84 83 82 81

Printed and bound in the United States of America.

Library of Congress Cataloging in Publication Data

Swinburne, Laurence.
  Riders on the wind.

  SUMMARY: Three men in a hot air balloon trace
Charles Lindbergh's solo airplane route across the
Atlantic.
  1.   Balloon ascensions — Juvenile literature.
2.   Transatlantic flights — Juvenile literature.
[1.   Balloon ascensions.   2.   Transatlantic flights]
I.   Hubrich, Dan.   II.   Title.
TL621.D68S94   629.13'091'1   79-21190
ISBN 0-8172-1568-9 lib. bdg.

CONTENTS

CHAPTER 1

For the Thrill of It

It was a little after 5:30 P.M. on Friday, August 11, 1978, when the helium gas started to flow into the huge flat bag on the ground. Slowly the bag began to grow and fill out. Then it rose, its silver tip lifting towards the still blue sky. The people who were watching gave a cheer.

The gas tanks kept on hissing and pumping helium into the bag. Now the black bottom of the bag appeared. The balloon had come to life! It was a beautiful sight.

A mile away, a farmer waved down the car of a friend. "John, what is happening down at Merle Sprague's fields?" he asked.

"Three guys are going to try to cross the Atlantic in a balloon, Andre," John answered. "They're going to take off from Merle's clover patch."

Andre whistled. "Now that's something. Nothing like this has happened in Presque Isle since

John Kennedy came when he was running for president. Give me a lift, will you please, John?"

As the car sped down towards Sprague's farm, Andre asked, "Think they'll make it, John?"

John shook his head. "No." He grinned. "They're crazy. It can never be done. Look how many people tried it already."

By the time they reached the clover field, the balloon was filled. It swayed in the light wind. The three balloonists were climbing into the cartlike box called a gondola, which was attached to the balloon by strong ropes.

Andre read the lettering on the side of the gondola. "*Double Eagle Two*. Now why do you think they named it that?"

"Because they tried to make it across last year in *Double Eagle One*. They dumped in the ocean. They were lucky to come back alive. You would think that was enough. But, no, here they are again."

"As you said, John," said Andre, "they're crazy."

Even though most people in the crowd agreed with John and Andre, they held their breaths as the balloon floated off the ground. There is something very beautiful about seeing a brightly colored balloon rise into the blue.

Then they got their voices back and they cheered. Shouts of "Good luck!" reached the balloonists' ears and they waved back. "Crazy all right," said John, "but they sure have guts." He watched *Double Eagle Two* shrink into a silver speck as it floated north towards Canada. "I wish I had half as much courage."

———

Have you ever wanted to do something no one else has done? Something dangerous? Something that doesn't have much point, but is done just for the sheer excitement of adventure?

That was the dream of Ben Abruzzo, Maxie Anderson, and Larry Newman. They knew that floating for more than 3,000 miles over the Atlantic Ocean wouldn't prove much more than that it could be done. In 1926, Charles Lindbergh had flown in a small plane from Long Island, New York, to Paris, France. That, too, had been a first, but it had been very important. It showed that airplanes could cross the ocean. It had been a big step in air travel.

Even then, it had taken only thirty-three and one-half hours. Today, airplanes that go much faster than the speed of sound make the trip in less than five hours.

If *Double Eagle Two* kept up its speed, the journey would take many days before it touched down in France—if it ever got that far. Even if the flight was successful, no one would begin signing up passengers for balloon trips from the

United States to Europe. If it wasn't successful, well, it would only be another failure in a long list of failures.

So the voyage was being done for the thrill of it and nothing else. That was enough. That is why people climb high mountains, go burrowing under the earth in endless caves or try to swim from Cuba to Florida—because these test their strength and, most important, their courage.

Certainly the three men didn't do it for money. In fact, just putting the balloon and gondola together and adding special equipment had already cost them $70,000. The total bill would be about $125,000.

They knew very well how dangerous the trip would be. For more than 100 years, people had been trying to cross the Atlantic in balloons. For the twenty years before the black-and-silver *Double Eagle Two* left Presque Isle, Maine, there had been eleven tries. Five people had died. The others had been pulled out of the ocean.

But the three men were sure that a balloon could make it to Europe. Only last month two Englishmen were almost in sight of France when they ditched, or went into the water. If they had managed to keep their balloon going for another 117 miles, they would have stepped off on land instead of onto a rescue boat.

The summer before, Ben Abruzzo and Maxie

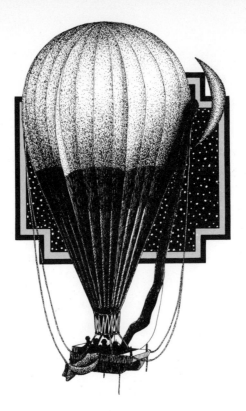

Anderson had also failed. They had gone about
two-thirds of the way and then had fallen into the
sea near Iceland. Abruzzo had sworn then that
he would never again go on such a foolhardy
adventure. His feet were so cold before the two
were rescued that he almost had to have them
cut off.

"You really mean you won't try it again,
Daddy?" asked his twelve-year old daughter, Pat.

"I promise you I won't," said her father. "I've
learned my lesson."

But Albuquerque, New Mexico, where Abruzzo lived, is considered the headquarters for

sport ballooning in the United States. On almost any Saturday or Sunday, the usually clear sky is dotted with dancing colorful balloons. It did not take long for Abruzzo to feel the old tug for trying the impossible again. Another time we might make it, he thought.

Maxie was ready, too. They decided, though, three passengers were better than two. Larry Newman jumped at the chance to join the crew. He hadn't been ballooning too long, but he was a trained airplane pilot.

They had taken off from Presque Isle, Maine, feeling confident. They would make it this time, they were sure.

But the sun soon left the sky. The stars stared down coldly at them. A quarter-moon crawled over the horizon.

In the darkness and silence of the lonely night, the men now began to wonder. Would they arrive in France, after all? Or would *Double Eagle Two* plunge them into the ocean where once again they would have to be rescued?

Or, worse yet, would they sink beneath the waves as so many had before them?

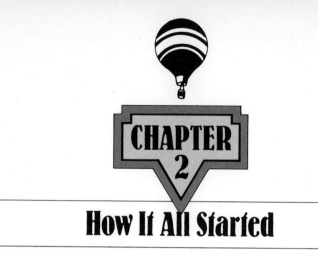

How It All Started

Many people are surprised to learn that balloons were the first method humans had to fly through the air. Ballooning has been with us a long time. Almost two hundred years of experience, of adventure, and sometimes of death had to take place before such a balloon as *Double Eagle Two* could be built.

For as long as anyone knows, people dreamed of moving like birds through the sky. A myth tells of a Greek, Daedalus, who was thrown in prison by the king of Crete. There seemed to be no way to escape. But Daedalus was a clever man. He and his son, Icarus, made wax wings. One morning the two flew out of their prison window and started towards their home in Greece.

Icarus, though, was excited by this new way of traveling. He flew too near the sun. Icarus's wax wings melted, and he fell into the sea and drowned. His father was not able to help him. Sadly, he flew on.

Another myth involves Mercury. He was a Roman god who carried messages. He had wings on his feet and his hat with which he could fly around the world in seconds. Another god, Apollo, drove the sun through the skies in a chariot.

These were just stories, but for hundreds of years there were many ideas for flying machines. Most of them had wings. Leonardo da Vinci, one of the world's greatest thinkers, drew a plan which showed a man pedaling through the air. This pedaling turned a propeller. It was a brilliant idea. DaVinci would have seen his idea come true in 1979 when a man actually did pedal through the air over the English Channel.

But flying was only a dream until 1783. In that year, two French brothers, Étienne and Joseph

Montgolfier made the first balloon—out of paper! Under it they built a fire, which filled the balloon with hot air. And away it went!

Soon many balloons were flying around France. Once one of them landed near a small village. The people there had never seen a balloon and they thought it was a monster from outer space. They attacked it, making holes with pitchforks. To make sure the "monster" was dead, they had a horse pull it along the ground for miles.

The development of the balloon was something like that of the space rocket. First the balloons were sent up alone. Then, to find out if ballooning was harmful to life, animals were put in a basket which was tied to the balloon and sent off. The first passengers were a rooster, a duck, and a sheep. The sheep got scared and stepped on one of the rooster's wings, breaking it. But on the whole the animals came out all right.

Now it was the turn of human beings. A young man named Pilâtre de Rozier volunteered to go. On November 21, 1783, he lifted off the ground before thousands of cheering French citizens.

Some of the crowd feared they were going to see a great accident that would kill de Rozier. But that didn't happen. He went up for twenty-five minutes and then came down. It was not long, but human beings finally had conquered the air.

De Rozier's airship was a simple craft. There was a small pot in the basket just below the mouth of the balloon. Straw was put into the pot and set on fire. From time to time, de Rozier would throw more straw into the pot and the balloon went higher. When he wanted to come down, he simply took away the pot and the warm air inside the balloon cooled.

These early flying machines were very dangerous and many people lost their lives when the paper balloons caught fire. De Rozier himself was killed.

Some balloonists were lucky, though. Now and then, the balloon didn't burn completely. What was left formed a kind of parachute, and the person floated to the ground. Because of this, parachutes were invented and attached to almost every balloon.

Balloons got better as the years went by. Many uses were found for them. For example, they became a war weapon. Soldiers would be lifted 1,000 or more feet into the sky in a balloon attached to the ground. They would then be able to look over the enemy lines. They would make drawings of what they saw, and then would be pulled back to the ground.

Until the First World War, it was very hard to shoot these balloons down. But after airplanes were brought into the fight, balloons of this sort had had their day. As soon as a spy balloon went up, a fighter plane was on it, spitting bullets. The balloon would explode, and the soldier would have to parachute to the ground.

Balloons still had their uses in war, though. In World War II, empty balloons were sent up. Between these balloons were nets. Airplanes usually didn't dare come too near because they might hit the nets and crash.

There were many attempts to make balloons more useful. They carried mail from one city to another. Passenger lines were set up. Even sending meat from Texas to New York was tried. But none of these worked too well. The problem was that balloons couldn't be counted on to arrive anywhere at a particular time. In fact, no one could even be sure a balloon would even arrive at the place it was supposed to go. Too much depended on the wind.

The invention of the airplane ended attempts to make the balloon useful. But interest in riding these giants of the sky never died. It was fun and exciting to float over the earth.

And there were still great adventures offered by balloons . . . which was why Abruzzo, Anderson, and Newman were starting off for Europe.

CHAPTER 3

Ready for Anything

Their fears disappeared quickly as the dawn came up from the east. Only a few hours before, that sun had come up over Europe. France did not seem so far away.

The first three days were fine. Nothing went wrong. They began to think that maybe they would have smooth sailing all the way across the great ocean.

From time to time, they thought about the earth below. So much was happening down there in the everyday world. The New York Yankees were gaining on the Red Sox. They would go on to win a pennant and world series. Somewhere wars were going on and people were being killed. A woman was trying to swim from Cuba to Florida.

But in the *Double Eagle Two*, floating along at about 13,000 feet above sea level, all this seemed far away. It was so peaceful and silent in the sky.

They were moving along at about thirty miles an hour, but they could not feel any motion. That was because they were traveling with the wind and at the same speed.

"Learn by your mistakes," is an old saying. Ben and Maxie hoped they were learning from what had happened on ther first trip. Then they had floated too far to the north. Now their route was further south.

Also, they had waited until the right weather for balloons appeared over the Atlantic Ocean. A storm was moving southeast from Greenland. Usually storms are bad for long-distance balloon journeys. But the three men figured they could ride on top of the storm because it was moving at

about thirteen miles an hour. The average storm moves at about twenty-four miles an hour. That would have been far too fast for *Double Eagle Two*, and it would have crashed.

Where did they learn this information? From a company in Massachusetts that keeps track of the weather. They kept in touch with this company by radio. They were not going to be surprised by sudden storms or shifts in the wind.

Double Eagle Two had been made especially for this long trip. The balloon, or envelope as balloonists call it, was not painted silver on top and black on the bottom simply because the three men liked the colors. Do you know how much cooler you feel on a hot day when you wear something white? You also feel much warmer when you wear something black. That happens with a balloon as well. During the day, the silver top of the balloon did not take in as much heat as if it had been painted some dark color. That meant that the helium did not become too warm, which could have made the balloon go too high. The warmer the helium is, the higher the balloon will go.

At night, this idea worked in reverse. The water beneath the balloon gives off warm air which rises. The black bottom of the envelope takes in this heat, keeping the balloon from coming down.

When the balloonists wanted their craft to rise, they threw ballast over the side. The less the balloon weighs, the higher it will rise. At the beginning of the trip, the *Double Eagle Two* carried 600 pounds of lead and 5,450 pounds of sand. This was ballast and would be tossed over before anything else.

The gas inside an envelope must be lighter than the air outside if the balloon is to ride through the skies. It works the same way as a cork on water. Abruzzo, Anderson, and Newman had choices of three gases. They chose helium, even though it cost more than the other two.

They could have used hot air. That is the easiest to make, and it is the cheapest. All they had to have was a propane burner below the open end of the envelope. That would heat the air inside. It would lift the balloon just the way warm air rises in your home. But it would not have lifted the *Double Eagle Two* as high as they wanted to go.

They could have also used hydrogen. But this gas catches fire easily. A hit from lightning or a careless spark might cause the hydrogen to blow up. Then the men would have fallen to the sea in a flaming gondola.

So it was with good reason that they chose helium. They felt very safe with this gas above them because it wouldn't burn.

However, suppose *Double Eagle Two* did fall. That was always the biggest fear. But they had prepared for it. An American satellite going around the earth kept an "eye" on the skyship. A radio beam was always going from the balloon to the satellite. If the balloon fell, the beam would stop. People in a station in Washington, D.C., would know right away *Double Eagle Two* was in trouble. They would also know where the balloon had dropped into the ocean. They could radio ships near the balloon to pick up Abruzzo, Anderson, and Newman.

If the rescue ship couldn't reach them quickly enough, the balloonists could make a sailboat out of the gondola. All they had to do was to cut away the ropes attached to the balloon. Then they could put up a mast and sails in the gondola.

It was little wonder that they felt so confident as they were ending their third day in the sky. They had been cold at night, but that didn't bother them. They had sleeping bags that kept them warm until dawn.

They were too confident. They were just about to run into trouble.

CHAPTER 4

Riders on Top of a Storm

The radio failed. They felt like kicking it or throwing it as far as they could out to sea. It had cost them a lot of money.

Lucky for them, they had brought along another radio. It was the kind used by radio "hams." If they had not had the second radio, they could have been pushed down into the ocean without warning.

But they did get warning. There was a sudden crackle over the radio set. Then they heard a faint voice of a man at the weather information company in Massachusetts. "Fellows, I'm sorry, but you've got to go higher. The very devil of a storm is coming straight behind you out of Canada."

"That's just great," said Abruzzo. But he meant just the opposite. "How high do you figure we'll have to go to get above it?"

"Up to at least 21,000 feet, but you don't have

to go higher than 24,000 feet," said the man in Massachusetts.

"Thanks a lot," groaned Larry Newman. "Why didn't you tell us about this storm before we started off?"

But the three men now far out over the Atlantic Ocean knew the answer. It was not the weather information company's fault. Figuring out what the weather might be is a tricky business at best. It had been almost four days since *Double Eagle Two* lifted from Merle Sprague's clover field. No scientist in the world could have known that a storm would have formed in Canada and chased the balloon.

However, they had to rise and that was all

there was to it. The news couldn't have come at a worse time of day. It was late afternoon. At sunset, balloons tend to go down a few hundred feet because the helium is cooling.

They began to throw over ballast. This was not a matter of just tossing bags of sand and lead bars over the side. It has to be done very carefully, a little at a time. If they rose too fast, they might go above 24,000 feet. If they didn't rise quickly enough, though, the storm would be upon them.

It took two hours to finish the job. By then, their teeth were chattering, and they were shivering. They had been cold enough at 13,000 feet. At 21,000 feet, the temperature was below zero.

What was even worse was that they didn't feel the wind, even though they were riding with it. It surrounded them, pushing its freezing breath through their jackets and trousers.

Their clothes were warm enough for an ordinary cold day back in Albuquerque, New Mexico. But they were not much help here above the clouds of the ocean.

There was a good reason for their light clothes. The year before when Abruzzo and Anderson had had to ditch, they found that the heavy jackets filled with down made them sink. It was all they could do to keep their heads above water until they were rescued.

Then there were the oxygen masks they had to

put on. The air is too thin at 21,000 feet to be able to breathe correctly. Without the masks, they could not have stood it for long.

Yet living in these masks was not easy. The oxygen made their mouths and noses very dry. Also, their voices changed to high pitches, making them sound like 33 rpm records being played at 45 rpms.

That wasn't the worst of it. It was hard to sleep. They were afraid that the oxygen tanks might spring leaks or that somehow the hoses might get clogged. If that happened, they would never wake up.

But they knew they had to rest and somehow they managed to sleep. Perhaps it was the thought that one was always awake and on watch that helped them close their eyes at last.

They escaped the storm. In the morning, the clouds swirled below the skyship. But ahead of them was the sun coming up again over the horizon.

Double Eagle Two had now traveled further than its twin had in the summer of 1978. In fact, the adventurers from New Mexico had gone further across the Atlantic Ocean than anyone else, except for the two Englishmen who had just missed reaching the British Isles by a few miles.

They did not know it, but the world had finally become interested in them and what they were

trying to do. Perhaps these three daredevils would succeed where so many had failed. No one would take seriously their goal of landing in France at exactly the spot where Charles Lindbergh had touched down in his tiny airplane fifty-one years before. If Abruzzo, Anderson, and Newman came to earth in Ireland, why, that was enough to win them praise everywhere.

But the three men were serious. They said they would land in France. They meant to do it. Their wives were already in England, preparing for a party they hoped would be in Paris.

Newspaper reporters rushed to Albuquerque to talk to the balloonists' friends. They discovered that all three ran very successful businesses. Ben Abruzzo built vacation parks. He was forty-eight years old. Maxie was forty-four. He owned copper mines. Larry Newman was thirty. He ran a factory that made hang gliders. In fact, he had a hang glider on the gondola. It was his aim to jump out of the balloon when it was ready to land and fly down to the ground.

"Why are they doing it?" asked the reporters, "It's not to make money and it isn't because they want to show off. Why?"

"Because they want to," was the usual answer.

One friend gave a grinning reply. "Because they are wild men!"

Well, they probably would make it if their luck held out, even though they were floating much higher than they wished, and they were freezing. It was already Wednesday. One more night and they should be drifting over land.

But they would be in plenty of trouble before that!

CHAPTER 5

Diving Towards Death

They thought their problems were through. Either at sunset or shortly after, they would be floating over Ireland. They were still shivering, and it was still a bother to wear oxygen masks. But the end, they believed, was in sight.

They didn't know they were coming near to a cold sink. A cold sink may happen suddenly. A kind of haze moves between the sun and a balloon. The helium cools quickly, and down the balloon goes! Even if the three men knew it was going to happen, there was little they could do about it. A balloon can't be steered. All it can do is drift with the wind. And in this case the wind moved them into the cold sink.

One moment they were looking down at the clouds below and thinking how beautiful the sun looked on them. The next second they felt as if they were in a whirlpool, twisting and falling fast.

Now their worry was not that they might not make Ireland. The situation was much worse. They might be pulled down into the water before they could radio for help. Of course, the space satellite would show the people in Washington, D.C., that they had ditched. But the speed of the crash might smash the gondola to pieces. They could very well be drowned before the rescue ship or helicopter arrived.

"Get rid of the ballast!" Abruzzo yelled. His two friends didn't even need the command. Already they were tossing the last bags of sand and the lead bars overboard.

But that wouldn't be enough. There wasn't much ballast to get rid of. "We were all scared," Abruzzo said later. *Double Eagle Two* was still falling fast.

Over went food and equipment. Even Newman's pride and joy, his hang glider, was pushed off. What next? They looked around. Then, as if the three men had the same thought at the same time, they took up axes. Smash! Bang! Crack! They were hacking large chunks out of the gondola. They threw the sleeping bags over, even though it meant they would be colder at night.

Yet down they kept going. Down and down and down towards possible death. It was like being pulled into a washing machine and not being able to do anything about it. The blanket of clouds below them could be their grave. If they got into the clouds, the helium would cool even more and they would fall faster.

But they were lucky. There was a hole in the clouds. It was a million to one chance that they would hit it. But they did! They could see the hungry waves below, but they felt a little safer.

Yet they kept on falling. They noticed, though, that the balloon was now coming down slower. At last *Double Eagle Two* stopped falling.

It hung 4,000 feet—about three-fourths of a mile—above the ocean. The sun beamed down on them. They slumped back, exhausted. If they drifted along in the cloud hole, they might come out of this all right.

The airship did stay in the hole. At last the envelope received enough heat to allow the balloon to rise to about 16,000 feet. The clouds drifted away. The sun went down behind them in the west in a blaze of color.

It was beautiful. The sun was their friend. Its heat warmed the helium and kept them at a safe level.

But when it turned dark, trouble came again. Ice formed on top of the envelope. They started to go down again, slowly this time. "Maybe we have sprung a leak," said Anderson.

No, said the others. They could see the ice. There was nothing they could do about it, however. They just hoped for the best and kept on looking ahead and down into the darkness. *Double Eagle Two* settled at 13,500 feet.

Some time after that, Abruzzo and Anderson, the old friends who had shared so many dangers, got into an argument. In the dark, they screamed at each other.

Larry Newman kept out of the fight. He knew the reason for it. Their nerves had been pushed almost to the breaking point. The argument was silly, but he knew better than try to break it up. It would just have to burn itself out. In a few minutes both men were silent, thinking of other things.

At ten o'clock that night, they saw tiny points of light below them. "Ships?" wondered Abruzzo aloud.

"No, I don't think so," said Newman. "Too many. More like houses. A town maybe."

He was too tired to realize the importance of what he had said. But Anderson was not. "Ireland!" he shouted. "We've made Ireland!"

They had done what no one else had been able to do. They had crossed the Atlantic Ocean in a balloon! Even though they couldn't see they pounded each other on the back and shook hands.

If they went down now, no one could blame them. But, tired as they all were, they decided to keep on to see if they could make it to France.

"And not only France, but Paris, France!" stated Newman.

He got on the radio. Stations in Ireland and England got his message. "We're here! *Double Eagle Two* has done it!"

The news flashed around the world. People were amazed. Back in Presque Isle, Andre the farmer heard about it on his car radio. He raised a fist and cheered. "And John said it couldn't be done!"

In Albuquerque, it was still early afternoon

when the word arrived of what three of its citizens had done. People ran out on the streets or phoned their friends. "Did you hear that Abruzzo, Anderson, and Newman are over Ireland?" The governor of New Mexico sent a message of congratulations to the three brave men.

But could they make France? Only time would tell.

CHAPTER 6

Touchdown

They only saw the electric lights of Ireland.
When the sun rose again, they were floating over
Wales.

A sailor in the British Coast Guard was the first
to see *Double Eagle Two*. He was on watch at a
beach station at dawn. He waved at the airship
even though he knew the passengers could not
see him, since they were more than two miles up.

"It was strange and beautiful at the same time,"
he said. "It was a silver pear upside down, and the
sunrise made it glow red and pink."

Everyone had to see it. People stood on streets
or their lawns, many in nightclothes.

Then the balloonists were over the English
Channel, which separates England from the
mainland of Europe. Abruzzo, Anderson, and
Newman were too excited to be tired now. They

stared out at the coast of France coming up as if it was a land they had just discovered.

Suddenly there was a roar coming behind them from England. "Hope that helicopter doesn't try to come too close," said Anderson nervously. "Sure would be a shame to come this far only to have our balloon blow up because it got hit with those propellers."

He didn't have to worry. The helicopter came near, but the pilot was careful not to put them in any danger.

"Who's that waving at us?" Newman asked, shading his eyes to see better.

"Hey, it's our wives," yelled Abruzzo. Everyone waved. After a few minutes, the helicopter flew away towards the French coast. "They'll be waiting for us in Paris."

But the three men met another problem when they reached France. However, it was the simplest problem of their long trip.

"Blast it, there's no wind," said Anderson.

They moved very slowly now. Only a small breeze kept them going towards Paris. When they passed over a racetrack, Newman said, "Maybe we ought to set down there."

Abruzzo laughed. "That will really scare the horses, right?"

The news had spread through France. It seemed to the men in the balloon that all the people in the country were following them on the highways. The roads were clogged with cars, trucks, and bicycles.

It was late afternoon. The Americans discussed what was to be done. "At the rate we're going,

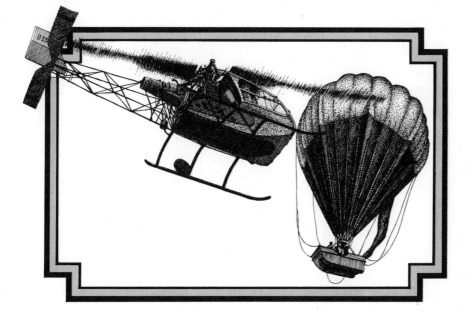

we'll never make Paris until tomorrow," Abruzzo said. "Who wants to go down right here?"

They had reached Ireland, they had reached England, and now they had reached France. It had been a long, dangerous, and tiring trip. They decided to go down.

"After all," said Anderson, "we're only about sixty miles from Paris."

They had started from a farm, and they touched down at a farm. They had started at sunset and landed at sunset. The only difference was that the American farm field had been growing clover. On the French farm, they landed in wheat.

It was over. The exhausted men climbed out and, for the first time in 5 days, 19 hours, and 3 minutes, they stood on solid ground. *Double Eagle Two* had traveled 3,120 miles through the air.

The balloonists expected a crowd, but they weren't prepared for what was going to happen. Thousands of people streamed across the wheat field. They mobbed the Americans. For a long time, Abruzzo, Anderson, and Newman had to sign their names to slips of paper held out to them. They talked to newspaper reporters and their pictures were snapped hundreds of times.

One old man stepped up to them and said, "I was at the airfield fifty-one years ago when

Lindbergh landed. I shook his hand then. I should like to shake hands with each of you now."

They might have been at it all night, but a helicopter swooped down from the sky. The pilot opened the door and waved for them to climb in.

In a few minutes they were in Paris and were taken to the American Embassy. There they hugged their wives, and shook hands with the people working there. Then they slipped into baths.

After soaking for an hour, they went to the party their wives had planned. They were three happy Americans. It all seemed so easy now . . . until they started to think about the cold and the falling and the gasping for breath at 21,000 feet above the ocean.

For the next few days, they and their wives were very busy. They met with many important French people. Everyone had a million and one questions. For a week, they were front page news. One of the Paris newspapers called them "The Wonderful Fools."

Then they flew to London, England. They met the two English balloonists who had almost been successful in their try to cross the ocean. There was no bad feeling between the two groups. Up in the air, all are brothers and sisters because they face the same dangers.

At last they headed home. For a long time, the three men looked out the airplane window at the sky they had conquered.

Finally Abruzzo said, "Remember that argument we had on the night before we reached land, Maxie?"

"I do remember something about it," answered Anderson.

"What was it all about, anyhow?" Abruzzo said.

Anderson shook his head. "I don't know."

Abruzzo laughed. "Neither do I." Then he became serious. "Listen, fellows, that first night we spent in Paris, I had an idea. I woke up sometime after midnight and couldn't get back to sleep for an hour. That's how good an idea it is."

They could see he was excited.

"What is it, Ben? asked Newman.

"Have you ever read that book, *Around the World In Eighty Days* by Jules Verne?" His friends nodded. "Well, the hero went part of the way by balloon. Now suppose we went *all* of the way by balloon. I figure we could do it in thirty days." He leaned back with a smile. "That would be something."

The other two men leaned back, too, thinking. Yes, it really would be something.

They might just do it, too.